This Little Tiger book belongs to:

_____

_____

_____

For my sister Pam, with love
~ P. B.

For Ravi, Patrycja, and
Mehrdad, with love ~ B. C.

LITTLE TIGER PRESS
1 The Coda Centre, 189 Munster Road, London SW6 6AW
www.littletiger.co.uk

First published in Great Britain 2006
by Little Tiger Press, London
This edition published 2013

Text copyright © Paul Bright 2006
Illustrations copyright © Ben Cort 2006

Paul Bright and Ben Cort have asserted their rights to be
identified as the author and illustrator of this work under the Copyright, Designs
and Patents Act, 1988

Printed in China • LTP/1900/0680/0613

2 4 6 8 10 9 7 5 3 1

Paul Bright

Ben Cort

I'm Not Going Out There!

LITTLE TIGER PRESS

I am underneath the bed,
Hardly poking out my head.
It's a squeeze and hurts my knees,
but I don't really care.
Can you guess, do you know,
Why I whisper soft and low?

I'M
NOT
GOING
OUT
THERE!

There's a dragon breathing smoke,
Who looks far too fierce to stroke,
And his eyes have got a scary sort of stare.
I hope he doesn't stay,
But he's not what makes me say,

I'M NOT GOING OUT THERE!

There's a ghost who's got no head,
With some toast and chocolate spread
Which I'm sure he would be very
pleased to share.
And even though I'd like a bite,
Still I'm keeping out of sight.

I'M NOT GOING OUT THERE!

There are witches, old and stubbly,
'Round a bath all hot and bubbly,
Busy washing all their dirty underwear,
Hanging panties up to dry,
But they're not the reason why

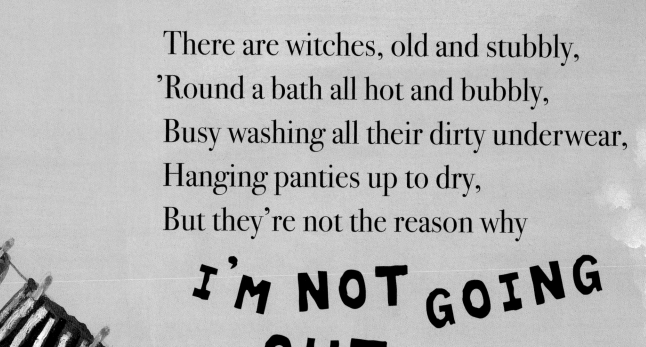

I'M NOT GOING OUT THERE!

There are monsters of all sizes,
Doing dancing exercises,
Wearing tutus, with pink ribbons in their hair.
And even though they look quite charming,
There is something else alarming;

I'M NOT GOING

Suddenly there's a shrieking—
And a squealing and a squeaking,
Loud enough to give the boldest beast
a scare.
Now I'm shaking and I'm quaking—
There's a noise of something breaking.

I'M NOT GOING OUT THERE!

The dragon turns quite pale,
From his nostrils to his tail.
While his dragon heart starts pounding,
Up the stairs he's flapping, bounding.
"Let's not panic!" gasps the ghost.
"Keep your head! Don't lose your toast!
I can haunt some other day,
Now I need to get away!"

All the witches spill their washing
And go splishing, splashing, sploshing,
Screeching spells to get things dried,
And to find a place to hide.
Hide from what? They'll soon find out!
They can hear it scream and shout.
Better hurry! Better run!
'Cause it doesn't sound like fun.

Even the monsters don't feel brave,
'Though they try hard to behave,
So they dance off in a row,
Each one on his tippy-toe.

Then all that I can hear,
Very loud and very near,
Is the thing that made them flee.
Do you know what it could be?

It has teeth that bite and gnash;

It has eyes that dart and flash.

We can hear it grumping, jumping,

Hear it stamping, stomping, thumping.

It has hands that pinch and snatch;

It has nails that claw and scratch.

It sounds ready for a fight;

We squeeze in and squash up tight!

There it is—my sister Kate!
And she's in a frightful state,
Making shrieking sounds,
and leaping in the air.
For, you see, she now knows who
Put the spider in her shoe!

I'M NOT GOING OUT THERE!